155849

AR 2.4
Pts 0.5

D1305068

Aa Bb Cc

Text and art copyright © 2004 by Max Lucado.

Story based on the characters from Max Lucado's *Hermie: A Common Caterpillar.*
Visit us at: www.hermieandfriends.com
Email us at: comments@hermieandfriends.com

Illustrations by GlueWorks Animation.

Published in Nashville, Tennessee, by Tommy Nelson®, a Division of
Thomas Nelson, Inc.

The publisher thanks June Ford, Amy Parker, Troy Schmidt, Holly Gusick,
Kathleen Vaghy, and Edna F. Ford for their assistance in the preparation of this book.

Library of Congress Cataloging-in-Publication Data

Lucado, Max.
  ABCs : based on the characters from Max Lucado's Hermie : a common caterpillar.
      p. cm. — (Buginnings)
  "Max Lucado's Hermie & friends"
  Summary: Handsome Hermie the caterpillar and his insect friends introduce the
alphabet as they march in a lively parade.
  ISBN 1-4003-0420-2 (hardback)
  [1. Parades—Fiction. 2. Insects—Fiction. 3. Alphabet.] I. Title.
  PZ7.L9684Abc 2004
  [E]—dc22   2004000466

Printed in the United States of America
04 05 06 07 08 PHX 5 4 3 2 1

Buginnings

ABCs

Based on the characters from Max Lucado's
Hermie: A Common Caterpillar

Tommy
NELSON®
www.tommynelson.com
A Division of Thomas Nelson, Inc.
www.ThomasNelson.com

Hurry, hurry! Hurry, please.
It's Hermie's Parade of ABCs.

See the alphabet marching by,
And me in my fancy bow tie.

What a parade! Me, oh, my!
26 letters going by.

Hurry, hurry! One and all.
Here they come—
    some tall, some small.

Hermie's
Parade of
ABCs

Marching letters **A** and **B**,
Starting now, stepping high.

Antonio **A**nt juggles **A**corns
In front of a **B**eautiful **B**utterfly.

Look! It's **C**, **D**, and **E**.
What wonderful fun stuff!

Caitlin **C**aterpillar scatters **D**elicate **D**aisies
In front of an **E**aster **E**gg wearing a red **E**armuff.

Tee-hee-hee-ha-ha
Tee-hee-hee-ha-ha

Tee-hee-hee-ha-ha
Tee-hee-hee-ha-ha

Tee-hee-hee-ha-ha
Tee-hee-hee-ha-ha

Gg

Ff

Marching **F**, **G**, and **H**,
Standing tall, strong, and brave.

Flo the **F**ly carries a **G**iggling **G**ift,
And **H**andsome **H**ermie, that's me, I stand and wave!

March on,
Letters I, J, and K.

Icicle Ice cream and Jolly Jellybeans,
A treat from a Kindly King for you today!

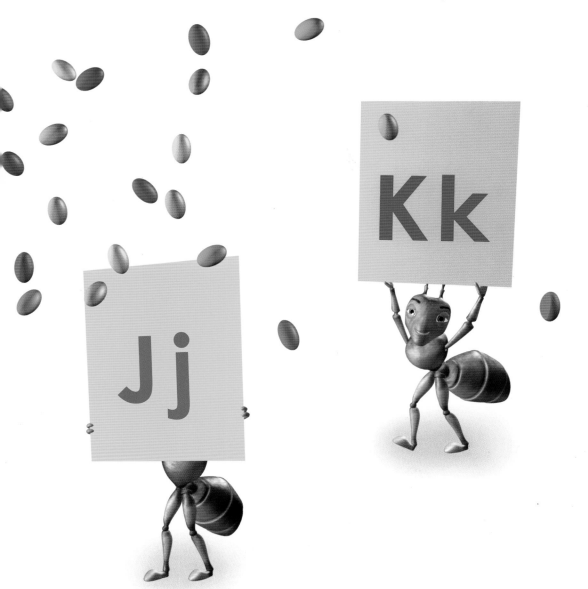

Marching **L**, marching **M**.
Look! We're halfway through.

Lucy the Ladybug and Messy Milt the caterpillar
Are waving a happy "Hello!" to you.

There go **N** and **O** and **P**!
And ants munching along the way.

Noodles and **N**uts, **O**nions and **O**ranges,
Peaches and **P**izza on a tray!

Marching along with **Q** and **R**,
The parade goes passing by.

The **Q**ueenly **Q**ueen flashes her **R**oyal **R**ing
As she waves a friendly "Hi!"

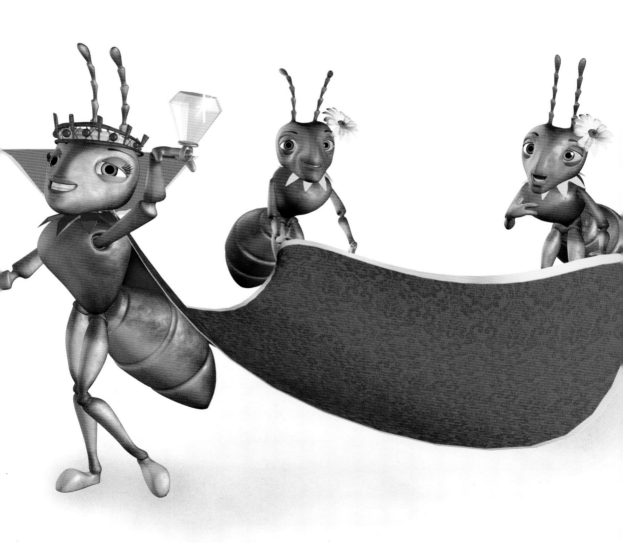

Marching with S, T, and U,
While the sun warms the ground.

Schneider Snail pulls a Toy Train of Unusual Umbrellas
To spread some shade around.

Marching, marching **V** and **W**.
I hear music in the air!

It's the **V**alentine **V**iolin
And the **W**onderful **W**ater Beetles with their **W**acky hair!

And now for letters **X**, **Y**, and **Z**.
We've saved the best for last!

It's an e**X**citing **X**-ray, Puffy's **Y**ellow **Y**o-**Y**o,
And the Ladybug twins' toy **Z**ebra **Z**ooming past.

Tee-hee-hee-ha-ha
Tee-hee-hee-ha-ha

Aa
Bb
Cc
Dd
Ee
Ff
Gg

Qq
Rr
Pp
Oo
Ss
Tt
Uu
Vv
Ww

Take your places, one and all.
Try to stand up straight and tall.
As I read your letters now,
Please step up and take a bow.